THE MONSTER WARDROBE

PAUL SHIPTON

Illustrated by Chris Smedley

OXFORD
UNIVERSITY PRESS

OXFORD

UNIVERSITY PRESS

Great Clarendon Street, Oxford OX2 6DP

Oxford University Press is a department of the University of Oxford.
It furthers the University's objective of excellence in research, scholarship,
and education by publishing worldwide in

Oxford   New York

Auckland   Cape Town   Dar es Salaam   Hong Kong   Karachi
Kuala Lumpur   Madrid   Melbourne   Mexico City   Nairobi
New Delhi   Shanghai   Taipei   Toronto

With offices in

Argentina   Austria   Brazil   Chile   Czech Republic   France   Greece
Guatemala   Hungary   Italy   Japan   Poland   Portugal   Singapore
South Korea   Switzerland   Thailand   Turkey   Ukraine   Vietnam

Oxford is a registered trade mark of Oxford University Press
in the UK and in certain other countries

British Library Cataloguing in Publication Data
Data available

ISBN-13: 978-0-19-918391-3
ISBN-10: 0-19-918391-0

3 5 7 9 10 8 6 4 2

Available in packs
Stage 13 More Stories A Pack of 6:
ISBN-13: 978-0-19-918386-9; ISBN-10: 0-19-918386-4
Stage 13 More Stories A Class Pack:
ISBN-13: 978-0-19-918393-7; ISBN-10: 0-19-918393-7
Guided Reading Cards also available:
ISBN-13: 978-0-19-918395-1; ISBN-10: 0-19-918395-3

Cover artwork by Chris Smedley

Printed in China by Imago

CHAPTER 1

Only for real monster lovers

No doubt about it, I thought to myself: *my little brother is an odd kid.*

Here's why. I had to write a story for English homework, but I couldn't think of a single idea. So Luke had given me one of his stories. It might spark off an idea for a story of my own, he'd said.

The problem is, all of the stories he writes are about vampires and monsters and mummies and nice things like that.

Like the story I had
in my hands now – it
was called *Night of
the Flesh-Eating
Spiders*.

I was up to the part where Brad
McSteel, the square-jawed hero, was
trapped in the attic by an oversized
spider from another planet.

I sighed and read what Mrs Hind,
Luke's teacher, had written at the end:

Very imaginative
as usual, Luke,
although it doesn't
really say much about
what you did over
the summer.

5/10

Poor old Mrs Hind! Imagine having
to read all these crazy stories by my
monster-mad brother! No wonder they
say teachers have got a hard job.

Just then there was a knock on my wall. It came from Luke's room and it was followed by a thin cry.

I threw the story down onto my bed and got up. I had a good idea what this would be about.

Sure enough, Luke was sitting up in bed. He had the covers pulled right up to his chin. The light was off, but the landing light was on and I could see the room fairly well. Luke's monster posters looked creepy in the half-light.

'What is it?' I asked, already knowing what the answer would be.

Luke raised a shaky hand and pointed towards the wardrobe.

There's a noise... I heard it.

His voice was as shaky as his hand.

It was coming from the wardrobe?

WOLFMAN

He nodded. A few days ago, Luke had seen a film about a monster that crept into kids' bedrooms. It lurked in the wardrobe and waited until the dead of night to pounce. Sure enough, Luke was now imagining that he could hear mysterious noises in his room at night.

On nights when Mum was home, Luke would shout for her when he got scared. But on nights like this, when Mum was working the night shift at the hospital – she's a nurse – Luke usually called me.

(Dad was in, but Luke had found that he wasn't very sympathetic. Dad just said that Luke's monsters were 'rubbish' and went back to watching TV.)

I strode over to the wardrobe and pulled the door open. I let out a gasp.

I gave him a smile. Like I told you, my little brother is weird. Even so, you can't help feeling a bit sorry for him. He just has an over-active imagination, that's all.

'Listen, Luke,' I told him. 'There's *nothing* hiding in the wardrobe. This is an old house, and old houses make a lot of noises. Floorboards creaking and stuff like that. That's all.'

I sat on his bed.

Why don't you keep the light on and read for a while? That always helps me get off to sleep.

Luke nodded and grabbed a book from his shelves.

'How about this one?' he said. 'I got it at a car boot sale with Mum this afternoon.'

He waved the book proudly.

My first thought was that he'd been robbed. The book looked as though it was going to fall apart. Then I glanced at the title: **BIG BOOK OF MONSTERS.**

There was no picture on the cover, but there was a sticker which said: **Warning. Only for real monster lovers.**

'That's not really the sort of book I had in mind,' I said. 'Haven't you got anything else?'

Luke stared at me blankly. I looked at his shelf full of horror and science fiction books and told myself not to ask silly questions.

Ok, then. But don't read for too long. Night, night.

CHAPTER 2

The wardrobe opens

Back in my own room, I wondered why
so many kids were so mad about
monsters. I mean, Luke was crazy about
them, but he wasn't alone in his
craziness. Lots of his friends shared his
strange interest in scary books and
comics. And I bet that, like Luke, they
ended up scaring themselves over
nothing.

I didn't understand it. Why like
something that makes you afraid?

Weren't there enough *real* things in the world to get scared about? Like whether you'd get a spot on the end of your nose. *Or* whether you could get your homework done on time.

Speaking of which... I picked up a pen and waited for a brilliant story idea to hop into my head.

I was still waiting and staring at a blank sheet of paper when the noise came again.

This time Luke was pale with fear. He fixed me with wide eyes.

What is it this time? It can't be noises from the wardrobe again?

I was snappy now. It was getting late and I hadn't even *started* my homework.

Luke shook his head nervously and pushed the book towards me. I glanced down at the open page.

The Monster in the Wardrobe

One of the most terrible monsters of all, this unstoppable beast only comes out to feed at night. It prefers to eat young humans, though it'll make do with adults if there's nothing else available. Able to see in the dark, it

I had read enough.

He pointed to the picture in the book. It showed a gruesome monster with a mouth full of jagged teeth.

The monster in the wardrobe.

That monster needs a good dentist, I thought to myself.

But Luke seemed really scared.

He stared at me. 'That picture... It's *my* monster. The one I can hear in my wardrobe. The one I have nightmares about... I don't understand how, but it's there in the book.'

I forced myself not to smile. I could see that he really believed all this rubbish and I didn't want to hurt his feelings. (I'm pretty good as big sisters go.)

So I thought carefully about what to say. I was still thinking when I heard the noise...

Just a quiet scraping sound at first.
It was coming from somewhere in the
room, near the end of the bed.

It was coming from the wardrobe.

A sudden chill gripped me. What if Luke was telling the truth? What if there really was...? I shook the thought from my mind and told myself not to be so daft.

And then the noise came again, louder this time. Luke was frozen in fear. My mind was racing. Maybe it was a mouse that had made its way into the house? Or perhaps something had gone wrong with the water pipes, or –

The wardrobe door began to creak slowly open.

And then something began to come out of it.

As if in a dream, I watched as a long, curved, SHARP claw slowly appeared around the wardrobe door.

A terrified croak escaped from Luke and my brain kicked into gear. I grabbed my brother by the wrist and yanked him out of bed.

RUN!

It seemed like the most sensible thing to do.

CHAPTER 3

Attack!

We didn't wait to see the rest of the thing that was in the wardrobe. No need – the sight of that fearsome claw had been more than enough. We ran for our lives and charged down the stairs.

Luke was still holding his book. He was clutching it as if it was going to save him.

I didn't have a plan, I didn't have a single thought except to GET OUT OF THERE AS FAST AS POSSIBLE!

I threw open the living room door to get Dad. The TV was still on – for some reason, even in my terror, I noticed that it was my favourite programme – but Dad was not in the room.

However, the room was not empty…

A giant hairy spider was bobbing up and down in front of the sofa.

When I say a *giant* spider, I don't mean one like you might see in the bath. I mean a GIANT SPIDER. Huge, enormous, gigantic. It was so big that its jet-black eyes were level with mine.

I heard a scream. It was a moment before I realized that it had come from me.

Luke and I ran back into the hall. A cry of rage followed us from the living room. It was the spider!

My brain didn't have time to puzzle over why there was a giant spider in our house. It was too busy trying to keep me alive!

If we could just make it to the front door...

Another enormous spider sprang out in front of us. Another set of eight hairy legs began to edge towards us. We were trapped!

Without thinking, I grabbed one of Dad's golf clubs from the hall. I held it in front of me like a sword. The spider didn't stop moving forwards, but it slowed down.

Then it let out a terrible hiss and charged. I reacted quickly (I'm an ace rounders player – my reactions are good). I whacked the creature right on the head. It leapt back in pain.

The first spider had now followed us into the hall.

I jabbed at it and this one stepped back too. I poked again, but it grabbed on to the club with its jaws. It was strong and it nearly managed to pull the club away from me.

My heart thudded in terror, but after a few long seconds I yanked the club free.

Luke, we've got to find a way out! I can't hold the two of them off for long.

But my brother wasn't listening. He was digging frantically in the chest of drawers behind him. At last, he pulled out what he was looking for – a water pistol!

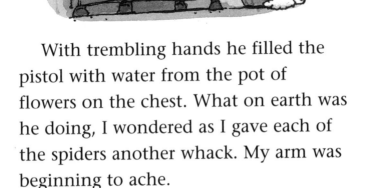

With trembling hands he filled the pistol with water from the pot of flowers on the chest. What on earth was he doing, I wondered as I gave each of the spiders another whack. My arm was beginning to ache.

Luke held the pistol out at arm's length and pointed it straight at one of the spiders. At that moment, my skinny little brother looked like one of those heroes he was always reading about in comics.

He squirted a jet at the spider. As soon as the water hit, the creature let out a shriek of agony.

There was a sizzling noise and clouds of foul-smelling smoke began to billow from the spider. The hall was filled with the horrible smell of burnt meat.

Within seconds the creature had dissolved to a pile of dust. It looked like a packet of instant soup someone had spilt on the floor.

Great!

Well, what else could I say?

The other spider bobbled nervously now and backed away down the hall. Luke stepped forward. I sensed a new confidence in my brother as he raised the water pistol.

He grinned as he pulled the trigger and... nothing. I followed Luke's horrified eyes down to the water pistol in his hand – it was empty!

But how? We could hear the *clump, clump* of footsteps on the stairs. Somehow this did not sound like the spiders' skittering legs. These steps sounded heavier, more threatening. It had to be the monster from the wardrobe!

We were trapped – the spider one way, the monster the other way. There was only one place to go.

Quick! The basement!

CHAPTER 4

The monster strikes

Luke's book was lying next to the chest of drawers. He'd dropped it when he was looking for the water pistol. I don't know why, but something told me to snatch it up now.

'Come on!' screamed Luke.
Luke and I raced for the basement.

We tugged open the basement door. As soon as we were inside, I checked the lock. Then I checked it again, just to be sure.

We ran down the steps.

In the dim light of the basement's single bulb, Luke and I looked at one another. Each of us knew what the other was thinking: we were trapped down there. Only one way in and one way out.

My heart was beating wildly. I forced myself to take a deep breath, and then I looked around for something else to use as a weapon.

There was an old exercise bike nobody ever used and some boxes of our old toys and outgrown clothes. Nothing we could use. I tightened my grip on the golf club.

A question made its way through the panic in my mind.

Hold on. How did you know that water would kill them?

An expression of terror and disbelief came over Luke's face. He said slowly, 'I knew because that's what happened in the story I wrote, *Night of the Flesh-Eating Spiders.*'

Of course, Luke's silly story about giant spiders from outer space! But how?

That's when I remembered what Luke had said about his book. His monster – the monster in the wardrobe – had been in that book. Could the spiders be in there too? I flicked through the tattered book in my hands.

I snapped the book shut as if one of the spiders could leap off the page.

Then I looked at the cover. The sticky label had begun to come off, so I peeled it away. The full title of the book could be seen now. Both Luke and I gasped when we read it: **LUKE McGUIRE'S BIG BOOK OF MONSTERS.**

How could my brother's name be on the cover? A chill did sprints up and down my spine.

Luke stared at me. 'I told you – at a car boot sale,' he said. 'The man who sold it to me said it was the perfect book for any kid who's into monsters. At first I wouldn't buy it, but he kept on dropping the price.'

I was baffled. This book was filled with all of the monsters from Luke's weird imagination. And somehow it was bringing them to life. But WHY?

I didn't have long to think the question over. Something new hit the basement door with a heavy thud.

BOOM! Then again, and again.

The other spider?

I shook my head. This was something bigger...

It had to be
the thing from Luke's wardrobe.

With the next thud came a different sound – the crunch of splintering wood. The door was breaking! The monster from the wardrobe was about to get in!

CHAPTER 5

Unstoppable!

What could we do? Panic clutched at my heart.

There was a terrible sound of shattering wood and bent hinges. The door was history. A scream tore from Luke's mouth. I looked up and saw a huge figure fill the open door-frame.

I got a glimpse of a snout as long as a crocodile's. Deadly teeth flashed – lots of them. A clawed hand reached for the light switch.

Then the light went out and everything was darkness. I could feel Luke huddling next to me.

A heavy footstep sounded as the monster began to come slowly down the stairs. *Thud.*

It was followed by a scraping sound as clawed feet dragged across the concrete steps. Then again – *thud, scrape.*

My mind was speeding. Think! What had the book said about this thing? The word came back to me like a splash of cold water – *unstoppable*. Whatever you did, this monster would get you in the end.

Somehow Luke's book was the key to all of this. I began frantically to rip out pages and scrunch them up.

I didn't know if it would work, but I didn't have any other ideas.

The beast was almost at the bottom of the stairs.

In the darkness it was impossible to see what page I was tearing out. I just kept on ripping. Sooner or later I'd get the page with the monster in the wardrobe. I HAD to!

A soft chuckle sounded as the monster reached the basement floor.

We were done for! Luke tightened his grip on me. I went on tearing up the book and throwing away the pages.

Even in the darkness I could see a bulky shape loom in front of us. A pair of yellow eyes glowed menacingly in the blackness.

Then – *rip!* – I pulled out one more page and there was a sudden flash of light in the basement.

The monster was surrounded by swirls of light. It let out a low, puzzled moan. Then the creature simply faded and disappeared. Soon all that was left was a pattern of stars dancing in the air.

And then nothing.

Luke's hand was still gripping my arm. I heard his voice in the darkness.

Before we did anything else, I ripped up the rest of the book. Whatever power it had, I wanted to make sure every bit of it was gone.

Then we nervously made our way up the stairs. We hardly dared to believe that it was all over.

I half-expected something to jump out at me. Nothing did. The place was a mess after our battle with the spiders, but the house was quiet.

We found Dad lying in the kitchen. He was asleep and I could see wisps of silky thread around him. I guessed that one of the spiders must have wrapped him up and dragged him in there.

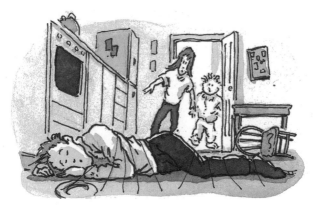

His eyes blinked open when we shook him. He looked pale but he was unhurt.

I started to answer, but then I stopped myself. Where to begin? I turned to my dazed-looking brother.

CHAPTER 6

The riddle of the books

It was the middle of the night but lights still blazed at the Darkwood Book Company.

In his office Mr Darkwood put the phone gently back on the hook. It wasn't good news. The book he'd sold to that boy, Luke McGuire, had been destroyed.

Darkwood stood and looked out into the night. Slowly he reached up and peeled the human mask from his face. That felt much better. To get things done, it was sometimes necessary to look like a human. But it always felt good to take the mask off.

He had not won tonight – but he knew there would be other chances.

And things were going quite well. Back in the old days, he had had to visit kids one by one. It had been fun but it wasn't the best way for a monster to carry out its task of spreading fear across the land.

Even monsters have to move with the times. So Darkwood had come up with this new idea of using the books. Now, he could work his dark magic far more quickly. He could scare hundreds of kids at the same time.

There was a timid knock at the door. One of his workers came in to the office.

Darkwood smiled.

About the author

When I was growing up
in Manchester, I always
wanted to be an
astronaut, a footballer,
or (if those didn't work
out for any reason)
perhaps a rock star.
So it came as something
of a shock when I
became first a teacher and then an
editor of educational books.

I have lived in Cambridge, Aylesbury,
Oxford and Istanbul. I'm still on the run and
now live in Chicago with my wife and family.

Years ago, my monster lurked on the landing
outside my bedroom. It never got me and
nowadays I sometimes wonder where it went.